Graham and Sandra met some 39 years ago and since had two children and three granddaughters. They currently live in the foothills of the Pyrenees in a small village in France. Up until recently they ran a boutique chambre d'hotes and also organise an annual cycling sportive, not for the fainthearted, that raises funds for bicycles for Africa.

THE PENELOPE, SEVI AND MIA
DETECTIVE AGENCY – BOOK 1
THE MYSTERY OF THE MISSING SOCK

G and Glam-ma

AUSTIN MACAULEY PUBLISHERS™
LONDON • CAMBRIDGE • NEW YORK • SHARJAH

A CIP catalogue record for this title is available from the British Library.

ISBN 9781398451575 (Paperback)
ISBN 9781398451582 (ePub e-book)

www.austinmacauley.com

First Published 2022
Austin Macauley Publishers Ltd®
1 Canada Square
Canary Wharf
London
E14 5AA

P S & M
T& L

This book is dedicated to our G
Graham Weeks
1958 - 2022

ALS for your encouragement
Austin Macauley for believing in us

It was Thursday morning, and sisters Penelope, Sevi and cousin Mia were watching Penelope and Sevi's mum do the weekly clothes washing.
"There are lots of clothes, Mum,"
said Penelope.
"Yes, I know and lots and lots of work,"
replied Mum.
Sevi whispered to Mia, "I don't think I will wash my clothes when I'm grown up."
"What will you do?" whispered back Mia.
"Let Mum do mine, she looks very good at it."
Mia thought about this for a while and agreed.
"Me too."
As Mum was sorting out another wash load, she sighed. "My word, for the life of me I don't know how that happens?"
Penelope was curious. "What
happens, Mum?"

Mum sagged onto a chair and smiled. "Well, Penelope, Mummy puts all the pairs of socks into the washing machine and when they are washed and I unload them, there is always a sock on its own, where has the other one gone? For the life of me I never know why."
Penelope turned to Sevi and Mia and said, "To the Wendy House, now."
At the Wendy House, Penelope announced, "We have a mystery to solve; we are going to find out where the missing socks are!"

Mia turned to Sevi and spoke softly, "But Sevi and I are just rug rats, how can we help?"
Penelope smiled. "Well, even Sherlock Holmes had his 'irregulars', I'm sure you and Sevi will be of great help and I declare that the 'Penelope, Sevi and Mia Detective Agency' is now officially up and running."
Sevi was a little concerned. "Err and what exactly are we going to do?"
Penelope puffed out her chest. "Well, first of all we will need a plan, a jolly good plan."
Mia asked, "And what will that be?"
Penelope frowned and said slowly, "Well err, one of us must watch the washing machine at all times whilst the other two distract Mum so she doesn't know what we are up to."

Sevi said, "Alright and when does this start?"
"Right now, the washing machine is on and running and so are we!" came the response from Penelope.
"Running?" asked Mia.
"Not actually running, but on, our way to solving the mystery of the missing sock."
It was Mia who had the first turn at watching while Penelope and Sevi kept Mum busy with constant questions and demands for sweets, cakes and biscuits, something they were
very good at.

Sevi went to do her watch of the washing machine. "Hi, Mia, did you see anything?"
"No, Sevi, and watching the washing machine is about as interesting as watching Dad at the golf range," retorted Mia.
And so Sevi started her watch. After about half an hour – well, it was actually six minutes but it felt like half an hour – a very strange thing happened.

A very small strange man, about 6"-high darted across the room and climbed into the back of the washing machine. Sevi was stunned and sat open-mouthed, staring at the washing machine. After a few minutes, the strange little man dressed all in green with a green pointed hat, came out of the back of the washing machine and sprinted off across the room and into the back garden; he was very fast and he was carrying a sock.

How to Catch a Thief

That night after bath-time, the three girls huddled in Penelope's bedroom. Sevi's discovery was very exciting and Penelope and Mia had quite a few questions for her.

- Where did he come from? I have no idea

- What was he doing? Stealing a sock

- What did he look like? Not quite sure he was very fast

But the most important question was

- How do we catch him?

"Cake," said Mia.
"Yes, please," said Sevi.
Mia sighed. "No, cake is how we catch him."
"Go on," urged Penelope.
"Well, he is too fast for us to catch him so we will put some nice cake down by the washing machine and when he stops to eat it, we will catch him in our fishing nets."
"Why cake?" quizzed Penelope.

"Who doesn't like cake?" said Sevi.
"Exactly," confirmed Mia.
Then Mum came in the room. "OK, what's going on with your three?"
"Nothing, why?" they all reacted together.
"Because there's no shouting, no arguing and no screaming, so I know you three are up to something."
"No, Mum, we are all good, honest Injun," said Penelope with her fingers crossed behind her back.
And then it was time for bed.

After three attempts, the cake had been squirrelled away; it had been so hard to save cake and not eat it when it tasted soooo good.
"We must remain still and quiet!" exclaimed Penelope.
"Then shut up!" retorted Mia and Sevi.
They waited with the cake by the back of the washing machine and their nets at the ready and waited and waited some more, then it all happened very quickly, very very quickly. As soon as the washing machine stopped, the little green man zapped into the back, came out with a sock and as he zoomed out, he scooped up the cake and then he was by the cat flap in the back door. He then stopped, turned to face the girls, took a bow and was gone.

"That went well," said Mia. "Oh and by the way, I was being sarcastic."

After a long pause, Sevi said, "What do we do now?"

"Plan B," proclaimed Penelope.

"What's plan B?" inquired Sevi with a slight frown on her face.

"Well," said Penelope, "I will tell you as soon as I have thought of it."

After some serious thinking time, Penelope announced, "OK, this little fellow is quite clever."

"And fast," said Mia.

"Yes and he's very quick," continued Penelope, "and as we will never be as fast as him we must be smarter than him."

"And how do we do that?" questioned Sevi.

"With Track and Trace."

"What's that?" asked Mia.

"Umm," continued Penelope, "it's something our government would like but can't find apparently."

"Yes and you have lost me too," frowned Sevi.

Penelope puffed out her chest and told them, "It involves cake, talcum powder and dad's binoculars," and then she sat down and explained her plan.

The next day, all three girls were ready and waiting for the mysterious magical mini-man.
Sure enough, as soon as the washing machine stopped churning the wee fellow appeared and flashed across the kitchen floor and into the washing machine, then out he popped into a tray of talcum powder deftly put in place by Mia, sped across to the cake placed by Sevi, picked it up, grinned and shot through the cat flap and darted across the garden all under the watchful eye of Penelope using Dad's binoculars.
Penelope proudly chimed, "Girls, I think we have got our man."

Sevi was doubtful. "Well, it doesn't look like we have much apart for a little
less cake." Unperturbed, Penelope said, "Don't you see? All we have to do is follow these white talcum powder footsteps and that will take us to our tiny sock snatcher."
"Brilliant!" congratulated Mia.
"Thank you," said Penelope.
The girls followed the tiny white footsteps across the yard and all the way down the garden until they stopped in front of a large old oak tree.
The white dabs went around to the back of the tree and stopped.

"Oh dear," said Mia.
"What now?" quizzed Sevi.
"Mmmm," Penelope pondered and then looked up the tree. "Look!" She pointed. "Tiny white dabs going up the tree, we must follow them."
"Must we?" asked Mia.

"Absolutely," acknowledged Sevi.
Penelope went off to the shed and returned with a step ladder that she place against the tree, thinking out loud, "This will get us up to that big branch and then we will see what we will see."
When the three of them climbed up the ladder, they all stood on a large branch. Where the branch met the tree, there was a long narrow slit where the white dust foot prints disappeared into.

Mia asked, "What do we do now?"
"Go in, of course," answered Sevi.
"OK, who's going first?"
"Me," said Sevi.
It was a tight squeeze but with a bit of a struggle, Sevi popped through the gap.
"Well, now it's our turn," said Penelope, walking to the gap.

Mia was last through and being the smallest didn't have too much trouble getting in. Once they were in, what a surprise they had.

It was the strangest place they had ever seen; it was a huge forest, the trees were purple and blue with leaves all the colours of the rainbow, a waterfall and a stream with bright silver water.

"What a strange place!" exclaimed Mia.
"You can say that again, I have never seen red grass before," added Penelope.
"Look," pointed Sevi, "the footprints go over to these bright blue rocks by the river." They followed the footprints to the rocks and saw that they ended at the water's edge.
"Oh the little man must have washed his feet in the stream and now we won't be able to track him anymore," Penelope said, sounding a bit annoyed.

"So what do we do now?" asked Sevi.
"Not a lot," came a squeaky high-pitched voice from behind them.

They all turned around and there he was, sitting on a pink rock, the strange little man and how odd he looked, dressed in green; green boots, green suit, green shirt and tie and a pointed hat, green of course. It wasn't only his hat that was pointed so were his ears, nose and beard – a green beard to match his green hair.

"What do you mean, not a lot?" demanded Sevi. "Well," said the green man, "you have so cleverly got yourselves here, in my world, but you will have to be extra clever to get back to yours," and with that, he ran away so fast it was almost as if he disappeared.
"What did he mean by that?"
asked Mia.
Penelope, scratching her head, replied, "Err the tree that we came into this odd land through isn't there anymore!"
Sevi cried, "If it's not here, how do we get back home?"

"That," said Mia, "is a very
good question."
The girls sat down despondently on a large
yellow boulder with blue spots and there was a
considerable silence which was eventually broken
by Mia.
"I'm hungry."

"I'm tired," said Penelope.
More silence and the Sevi stood up and said, "I'm
going to find that green mean man and bash his
head with a blue stick until he tells us how to
get home."

"Sounds like a plan, except the bit about the stick," answered Penelope.

Sevi stood up and continued, "We must start looking for him now, not just sitting here, looking sorry for ourselves."

"And find something to eat," added Mia.

"After I get that little man to tell us how to get home, I will cook him for you, Mia."

"No, thanks, Sevi, cake will do."

With that, the three girls got up and started walking through the magical and mystical world, not quite sure what exactly to do.

Meet Russ

The girls walked through fields of orange corn,
past a golden lake with blue- and-white-striped
flamingos and down a winding lane with purple
trees that had black leaves.
"We're tired," said Penelope.
"We're hungry," said Mia.
"We're lost," said Sevi and indeed they were lost,
in a land they knew nothing about, well and
truly lost.

They had seen some very strange things since
climbing through the tree but as they came around
a corner, there was the oddest sight they had ever
seen. Sitting in a deck chair, reading a newspaper
was a six-foot, red, white, blue and orange parrot
with a pink bowler hat on his head, the three girls
all stopped and stared at the parrot
open-mouthed.

The parrot lowered his newspaper, took off his reading glasses and said, "What's the matter, haven't you ever seen a parrot before?"

"Not wearing a pink bowler hat," said Mia.
"And not reading a newspaper," said Sevi.
"And never one who talked to us," said Penelope.

"Well, you have now," said the parrot and lifted his newspaper back up and carried on reading.

Penelope decided that they had got off to a bad start with the six-foot newspaper-reading parrot and maybe a little tact and diplomacy was called for so she did a small cough and said, "Erm, I wonder if it would be OK to ask you a few questions, Mr Parrot?"

The parrot slowly put down his newspaper and removed his glasses, smiled and said, "The name's Russell, but you can call me Russ and yes, you can ask me some questions but first, would you like some tea?"

"Ooo, yes please," responded Sevi and Mia together.
Russ pointed to the front door of his bright green cottage and said, "Well, we all better go inside then."

Russ's cottage was very comfortable and they all sat in a big pumped-up cushion with a brown flower pattern. Russ made blue tea in a large gold teapot and asked, "Would anyone like some cake?"

"Oh, yes please," chimed Sevi, Penelope and Mia. Penelope really wanted to ask Russ some questions although her mum had taught her that being polite went a long way to making people like you and if they liked you, they were more likely to answer your questions.

So when they all had a cup of tea and a slice of cake, Penelope asked Russ, "This is such a lovely cottage, how long have you lived here?"
"Oh," replied Russ, "you're not from 'round here, are you?"

"Oh Russ, we are a long, long way from home. How did you know?"
"Because here we don't have time; nothing gets old, it's the same time all the time, for ever and ever. You are from the human world where all they talk about is time and the weather."
Penelope thought about this for a moment and then asked Russ, "Russ, do you know how to get back to our human world?"
"That," said Russ, "depends on how you got here. How did you get here?"

Sevi piped up, "We followed a little green man through a tree, a little man so big dressed all in green with green hair and a green beard."
"Oh that's not good," Russ frowned.
"Why?" asked Mia.

"The green man you followed is Ozzy Orange."
Penelope interrupted, "Orange?"
Russ raised his wing to stop Penelope and continued, "Yes, I know, but let's not go there just at this moment. Ozzy is not a very nice individual, he is quite mean and worst of all, he works for a dark wizard called Frankie Fish-Face Salmon. Now you know who got you into the world of magic and only he knows how to get you back. He knows the way he goes into the human world and you will have to get him to tell you."

"Fine," said Sevi, "we will capture him, hold him down and I'll tweak his nipples until he tells us."
"I don't think that is a good idea,"
interrupted Mia.
"OK," conceded Sevi, "I'll tickle him until he says Uncle Percy and tells us."
Russ told them to calm down and then he told them what they must do. "I am going to give you a map."

"Oh good, buried treasure," said
Penelope gleefully.
Russ frowned and continued, "No, not buried
treasure, a map that will take you to Flamingo
Island where there are thousands of flamingos
and you must find a flamingo called Flo. Flo is
all-knowing and will be able to tell you how to find
Ozzy Orange and how to get him to tell you how to
get back to the human world."
Mia thought for a second and said, "How will we
know which one is Flo if there are thousands
of them?"

Russ smiled and replied, "That's easy, you know
all flamingos are blue with white stripes except
Flo; Flo is the only pink flamingo in the world."
"Erm," said Mia. Penelope shook her head at Mia
to stop her saying any more.
"Imagine a pink flamingo, who had ever heard of
such a thing?" said Russ.
"Well, I never," said Penelope with her fingers
crossed behind her back.
After a delicious supper of blue bananas and
orange sausages, they all had an early night, ready
for their adventure the next day.

Flamingo Island

Sevi was holding the map and staring at it with a frown. "This map makes no sense whatsoever." "That's because you're holding it upside-down," pointed Mia.

After turning the map the right way up, the three girls saw that they would have to go through Penguin Wood, up and over Cheese Mountain and then cross Flamingo Lake to Flamingo Island.

Russ had given them a large picnic hamper and sturdy walking canes.
"How long will it take?" Penelope had asked Russ.
"We don't have time."
"You don't have time to tell me how long it will take?"
"No," said Russ, "we just don't have time here, I've already told you that."

So, apparently with all the time in the world or none depending on how you looked at it, they set off for Flamingo Island. Penguin Wood was very beautiful and everywhere you looked there were penguins. Penguins fishing, swimming, playing games, dancing and they all appeared very happy indeed. Getting through Penguin Wood was not much of a problem; however, when they got to the end of Penguin Wood, they were faced with Cheese Mountain.
"It's very big!" exclaimed Mia.
"It's very steep," pointed Penelope.
"It's awfully smelly," sniffed Sevi.

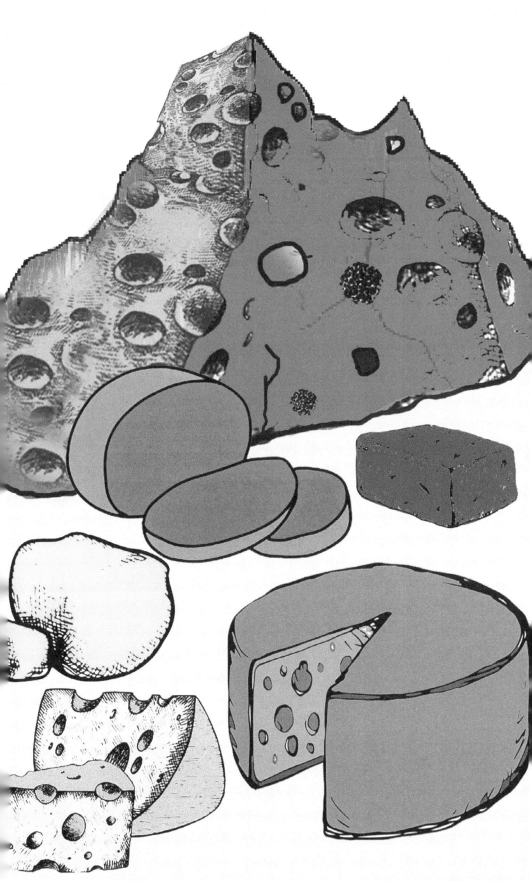

"Yes, it is," said Penelope. "What is that smell?"

"CHEESE!" they all shouted.

As they climbed Cheese Mountain, they were surrounded by large brightly coloured rocks that were all made of cheese; pink Cheddar rocks, green Edam rocks, black and blue Stilton and every cheese of every colour.

"Can we rest for a while?" inquired Sevi.

"Yes, let's and I'm hungry," said Mia, so they sat down on some orange Emmenthal rocks that were quite comfy and opened the hamper that Russ had packed for them.

"This is odd!" exclaimed Penelope.

"What?" the other two asked.

"Well, there are plates, knives, forks but only buttered bread and pickle to eat." After a small pause for thought, Penelope continued, "If only we had some..."

"CHEESE!" shouted Mia and Sevi and they all burst out laughing and started cutting big chunks of cheese out of the cheese rocks and made delicious cheese and pickle sandwiches.
After lunch, they climbed in much better spirits, being well-fed and rested. When they finally got to the top of Cheese Mountain, they had a magnificent view of Flamingo Lake and Flamingo Island.

The descent from Cheese Mountain was as hard as the climb up and it was three very worn-out girls who arrived at the edge of Flamingo Lake.
"It's a big lake," said Sevi.
"It's a strange orange colour," Mia pointed out.

"What isn't strange in this kaleidoscopic place," muttered Penelope.
"Kaleidoscopic?" asked the others.
"Colourful," clarified Penelope.
"Oh yes, it is that alright. How are we going to get to the Island?"
questioned Mia.
"We could swim," shrugged Sevi.
"It's too far for me to swim," said Mia, looking downcast.

They sat down on a large log of purple Comte and tried to think of a solution to their problem. After a while, Sevi asked, "Does cheese float?"
"Only one way to find out," said Penelope jumping up.
So the three girls rolled the huge purple log of Comte to the water's edge and together they chanted, "One, two, three, push," and rolled the cheese log into the water.
They waited a while and noticed that it hadn't sunk. "We should put our arms around the cheese log and paddle with our legs," said Mia, and so they did.

The water was quite warm and pleasant. Penelope was the strongest swimmer and the only problem they had was because Penelope was sitting on the left side of the log, it kept turning right, Mia suggested that Penelope went in the middle of the three girls and after that, all was well and they soon reached the edge of Flamingo Island where they were met by hundreds of blue with white striped flamingos.

Sevi turned to Mia and said, "How do we find the pink flamingo?" and one of the flamingos turned 'round and said, "You could just ask one of us to take you to her!"

"Err that would be very kind," said Sevi.

"Follow me," said the flamingo.

The girls walked alongside the flamingo and told him their names and the flamingo introduced himself as Bertram. "But you can call me Bert." After walking through lots of very tall purple grass, they came to Flamingo Town. The houses were all egg-shaped and were painted bright shiny colours. In the centre of town, there was a huge golden egg much bigger than all the other eggs.

Bert pointed to it and said, "There you go, that is Flo's house. Do you want me to take you in?"
"Yes please," said the girls.
They went up to Flo's front door and Penelope lifted the huge door knocker. Knock, knock.
"Wow, that was loud," said Mia.
"It's a big house," said Sevi.
After a short while, the door was opened by a very tall pink flamingo who said, "Hello, Bert, who are these people you have brought to
my house?"

"We are three girls and we are trying to track down Ozzy Orange who has stolen something that belongs to us and we would very much like your help if you don't mind," the girls chanted.
Flo smiled and said, "Then you had better all come in and we will have some pink pineapple juice and you can tell me all your problems and I will see if I can help."

The inside of Flo's house was pink; pink carpet, pink walls, pink furniture, pink curtains, pink, pink everywhere.

Mia whispered to Sevi, "I bet I can guess her favourite colour."

"I'm sorry, did you say something?" asked Flo.

"Er you don't have to go all that trouble," Mia said turning a little red in the face.

Penelope, giving Mia a little kick in the ankle, said, "Oh, thank you, Flo, we are so far from home in this place that is so strange to us. We really could do with some help."

"Nonsense, that's what I do, help people. Now, I will pour the pink pineapple juice and you tell me everything that has happened."

Penelope told Flo about Mum and the missing socks and the funny little green man and how they followed him and about Russ and well everything and "Now we are sitting here with you," finished Penelope.

Flo heaved a long sigh and then said slowly, "I think this is a three-pink-pineapple-jugs problem. Ozzy Orange is one very dodgy individual; although, Frankie Fish-Face Salmon is altogether a much meaner and nastier problem. Will you three have dinner with me and stay the night and tomorrow morning, I will tell you what can be done."

"We would love to," said Mia, "but I think our mums are going to start to miss us, we have been gone a long time."

Flo smiled and said, "We don't have time here, Mia. When, if, we get you back, then it will be at the exact same time as when you left."

They then had a superb dinner of all things pink; pink pears, pink ice cream, pink chocolate and lots of pink pineapple juice but later when they were all tucked up in a giant pink bed, Sevi said, "Are any of you worried that we will never get back?"

"A little," whispered Mia.

Penelope sat up and said, "I don't care how mean Ozzy or Fish-Face are, we are going to find them, sort this mess out and get back home."

"I hope you're right," said Mia and Sevi.

Penelope replied, "Of course I'm right, I'm always right, now let's get some sleep. I think tomorrow will be a very long day."

"Can you have a long day in a land that doesn't have time?" whispered Mia.

Penelope replied tiredly, "I really don't know. Goodnight, love you both loads," and turned out the pink light.

Flight Time

The next morning at breakfast, pink eggs on pink toast on a pink plate, Flo told the girls of her plan.
"Frankie Fish-Face Salmon hides out in the caves of the black mountain, it's quite a way from here but that's not a problem. When we get there, I will ask Frankie nicely to get Ozzy to tell you how to get you back."
Penelope frowned. "And what if he refuses to tell us?"

"Then I will ask him not so nicely," Flo replied.
So after breakfast, washed down with pink tea, they all climbed up the great staircase to the top of Flo's house and onto the roof.
"What happens now?" asked Sevi.
"We fly to the black mountains," replied Flo.
"Err we can't fly," laughed Mia.
"No, you can't, but I can and so can Ryan," Flo told them.
"Who's Ryan?" they asked. Flo turned around and pointed her wing up to the sky and said,
"That's Ryan."

44

The girls turned to look up to the sky and saw the biggest blue and white flamingo they had ever seen.

"Wow, Ryan is huge!" Penelope exclaimed and then Flo explained that the three girls would get on Ryan's back and he would fly them to the black mountain, about an hour's flight.
"Cool, that sounds like fun," laughed Sevi.
"Is it safe?" asked Mia quietly.
Ryan's deep booming voice said, "I have had as many take-offs as landings so I reckon you will all be OK with me."

The girls climbed on Ryan's back and then he started to flap his enormous wings and up in the sky they flew with Flo alongside.
Soon, Flamingo Island was a small spec in the distance and they were flying over dark blue and red trees and bright yellow rivers.
"This is fun," Sevi shouted.
"I think I prefer being inside an aeroplane with on board entertainment and refreshments," Penelope yelled back.

Ryan turned his head and asked Penelope what sort of bird was an aeroplane and she thought about it for a while and just said, "A big silver bird."

After about 50 minutes, they could see the black mountains in the distance and as they approached, everything became much darker, much, much darker and as they were about to make their descent, a huge black ball shot past them and then another and another.
"We're under attack," shouted Flo. "Quick, turn around and get back out of range."

Penelope looked down to the ground and saw lots of little green men loading the big black balls onto catapults and firing them at Flo and Ryan. Ryan was making a big sweeping turn when one of the balls hit his left wing and exploded, covering the girls in what tasted like water melon. Ryan cried out in pain and began to lose height, a lot of height very quickly.
"Ryan, are you alright?" Penelope asked, gripping on as hard as she could.

Ryan began to flap his bruised wing and started to slow down. "They hit me with a black water melon, it hurts but I will get us down safely and then rest."

"Look," pointed Mia. "There's Flo on the ground near those blue bushes."
Ryan said he could see Flo and made a slow and painful landing by her. Flo looked angry and almost shouted, "Those nasty little elves, when I get hold of Fish-Face, he's going to have some explaining to do."

"They are elves?" queried Mia.
"Working for Fish-Face?" asked Sevi.
Flo calmed down a bit and sat down and said,
"Yes, they are bad elves and they do Frankie's
bidding, but why they would attack us I have no
idea. Ryan, you must stay put and have a rest,
I will take the girls through the wooded maze to
Fish-Face's lair."

Ryan frowned. "Is that wise, I mean that maze is a
tricky place and probably full of Ozzy's
little friends."
Flo smiled and replied, "I can be a bit tricky too."

The Wooded Maze

When Flo and the girls arrived at the Wooded Maze, the girls were amazed. It was as high and wide as you could see and the trees grew in all directions, making tunnel paths going each and every way.
"Wow!" said Sevi.
Gulp, thought Mia.

Penelope turned to Flo. "Flo, how are we going to get through this maze; there must be thousands and thousands of different routes to follow."
"Millions." Flo smiled and there was a long silence before Penelope said, "So do we have a big problem here?"

Flo looked down at Penelope. "Not a lot of people know this but flamingos can fly 600km in one night and can fly up to 4.5km above the ground."
"And um how exactly does that help us?"
"Ah sorry, you see, we are great flyers and migrate so we have built-in directional radar."
"What does migrate mean?" whispered Mia to Sevi.

"Fly long distances to warmer places," Sevi whispered back.
"Oh, like going on holiday to Tenerife?"
"Yeah, sort of."
Flo told them to pay attention and stick close and follow her. Climbing through the maze was hard work and soon it became very dark. Flo had a pink torch that shone a bright pink light. They climbed, twisted, turned and fell occasionally.
Penelope turned to Flo. "We are all very tired, is it much further?"

"Not long now, just hang in there."
After a while the woods became a little lighter with beams of light shining through the dense branches here and there.
"Look," pointed Mia, "I think that is the end of the maze down there."

They climbed down and down to the wooded floor and eventually out into the sunshine and it was then they realised all was not well.
They were surrounded by hundreds and hundreds of little green men some holding bow and arrows and some long (well long for them) spears. At the front of all the green men was someone they all knew; Ozzy Orange.

Flo puffed herself up to her full height and growled at Ozzy, "Mr Orange, what is the meaning of all this?"
Ozzy stared back. "You will see soon, now just come along with us and no funny business."
The army of elves surrounded Flo and the girls and marched them down a bright blue road that meandered through a forest of yellow and blue trees.

Penelope whispered to Flo, "Where do you think we are going and what are they going to do to us?"

Flo turned to Penelope and whispered back, "My bet is we will soon be seeing Mr Fish-Face, although what they are up to I haven't a clue."
Flo was soon to be proved right; when they arrived at a village full of small pointed houses and buildings, the girls and Flo could see over the tops of all the buildings and could see at the centre of the town square a rather large fish sitting on an indigo coloured throne.
Sevi asked, "Is that...?"

Flo interrupted her, "Yes, Sevi,
Mr Fish-Face himself."
"Frankie, what are you up to and what is all this
nonsense about?" Flo challenged Fish-Face.
"None of your business," he sneered.
"It is my business when you attack me and my
friends with black water melons and now hold
us here."
Frankie's eyes narrowed and then after a pause
said, "I am not going to tell you. Ozzy, you and
your elves take Flo and her friends to the deep
mud pit and leave them there."

As the elves started to close in on Flo and the
girls, there was a strange whoop whoop whoop
noise that was getting louder and louder.
"What on earth is that sound?" Mia cried looking
up to the sky.
"Pat," replied Flo.
"Pat, who is Pat?" questioned Sevi.
Flo smiled. "A pat, Sevi, is the collective noun for
a group of flamingos."

They all looked up to the sky and as the sound grew louder and louder, they saw in the distance flamingos, lots and lots of them. Soon the whole sky was full of them, being led by an enormous flamingo called Ryan.

The flamingos swooped down and picked the elves up by the scruff of their necks and then flew to the mud pit and dropped them in it. In a very short time, all the elves had been rounded up and all that were left were Frankie and Ozzy. Ryan flew down and smiled at Flo.
"My wing was sore but I knew that you might need some help so I flew back to the island and got some."

Flo smiled back fondly. "Thank you, Ryan, that was very brave and very kind."
"Yes," agreed Penelope, "thank you very much and you saved us from having a mud bath too."

"Think nothing of it, but what are we going to do with these two scoundrels?"

Penelope bravely turned to Frankie. "Yes, Mr Fish-Face, we want some answers to some questions and we want them now."

"And the first question is," interrupted Sevi, "why are you stealing socks from my mum's washing machine?"

Frankie slumped down on this throne and said, "If you must know, it's because of the terrible way you humans treat our planet, you destroy so much of it just for your own pleasure and someone has to stop you."

Mia was quite perplexed. "But how does stealing socks do any good?"

"I think," acknowledged Flo, "that I know the answer to that. You see, if you have a piece of someone's clothing, you can use it to put a spell on them."

Frankie snarled, "Yes, when we have a sock from every human, I'm going to put them all in a sleep spell and stop them from damaging the planet."

Penelope came forward and said, "Oh dear Frankie, that is a little harsh, isn't it? I'm sure we could work something out without putting the whole human race to sleep."

"Like what?" Frankie demanded.

"Well, we are not all bad, there is Greta Thunberg, she is trying to do good and get everyone to tidy up, isn't she?"

Frankie sighed. "She's one of ours."

"What!" Sevi exclaimed.

Flo sat down and said, "Yes, it's true, she's a fairy. We sent her up to try and talk some sense into the humans, we put her in a human body we made."

Frankie added, "And you don't listen to her, so I set my own plan in motion."

Sevi looked at Flo and asked, "Why don't you just go to the human world and tell them, Flo?"

"Because grownups cannot see or hear us, because they are so sensible."

"Oh dear," said the three girls.
There was a long silence while everyone thought what could be done. Eventually, Penelope said, "OK we know that something must be done to clean up the world, we will go back and tell all our friends and they will tell all their friends , then when we become grownups, we will do what is right and what needs to be done."
Flo turned to Frankie. "Sounds like a better plan than yours, how about it?"

Frankie looked at Penelope. "It doesn't look like I have much choice but I'm still going to take socks so if when you grow up and you don't do the right thing, it will be sleep time for you all."
"WE WILL!" shouted the girls.
They then agreed that that's what was going to happen. Ryan and the Flamingos got all the elves out of the mud pit, all looking well, muddy but happy. It was agreed that the next day, Ozzy would take them back to the human world but first, they were going to have one great big party, so they did.

Home

Back in the kitchen, Mum was emptying the
washing machine when the three girls walked in.
"I don't believe it!" said Mum.
"What?" they asked.
"Another sock has gone missing," sighed Mum.
Penelope turned to Mia and Sevi, smiled and gave
them a big wink. "I wonder where it went?"

THE END

Lightning Source UK Ltd.
Milton Keynes UK
UKHW052004050922
408399UK00013B/247